LITTLE WOMEN

LITTLE WOMEN

Adapted by
LAURIE LAWLOR

from the Screenplay by
ROBIN SWICORD

Based on the Novel by
LOUISA MAY ALCOTT

NEWMARKET PRESS
NEW YORK

94 95 96 97   10 9 8 7 6 5 4 3 2 1

Library of Congress Cataloging-in-Publication Data

Lawlor, Laurie.
    Little women: the illustrated storybook for children / adapted by Laurie Lawlor from the screenplay by Robin Swicord; based on the novel by Louisa May Alcott.
        p. cm.
    Summary: This version of the classic story of four sisters in nineteenth—century New England is based on the Columbia Pictures movie.
        ISBN 1-55704-216-0
    [1. Family life—Fiction. 2. Sisters—Fiction. 3. New England—Fiction.] I. Swicord, Robin. II. Alcott, Louisa May, 1832–1888. III. Title.
PZ7.L4189Li 1994   94–37412
  [Fic]—dc20   CIP
                                                                      AC

Quantity Purchases
Companies, professional groups, clubs, and other organizations may qualify for special terms when ordering quantities of this title. For information, write Special Sales Department, Newmarket Press, 18 East 48th Street, New York, NY 10017, or call (212) 832-3575.

Book design by Tania Garcia
Half title art by Lauren Allard, Oakland, CA

Manufactured in the United States of America

First Edition

"I am in the garret with my papers round me, and a pile of apples to eat while I write my journal, plan stories, and enjoy the patter of rain on the roof, in peace and quiet. Being behindhand, as usual, I'll make note of the main events up to date, for I don't waste ink in poetry and pages of rubbish now. I've begun to *live*, and have no time for sentimental musing.... My book came out; and people began to think that topsy-turvy Louisa would amount to something after all, since she could do so well as housemaid, teacher, seamstress, and storyteller. Perhaps she may."

—Louisa May Alcott
(from her journal in April 1855,
when she was 23 years old)

(The book Louisa May Alcott refers to is Flower Fables, *which she wrote for Ellen Emerson, Ralph Waldo Emerson's daughter. The book was her first official publication—a collection of fables with flowers for characters—published on December 19, 1854.)*

CHAPTER ONE

Christmas 1863

Long ago there lived four sisters, not one of them alike. The eldest, eighteen-year-old Meg, was as fair and prim as a turtledove. Next came seventeen-year-old Jo, strong and wild as a sea gull that flies into storm and wind. Fourteen-year-old Beth, shy like a peeping dull-colored sandpiper, never strayed far from home. Last came twelve-year-old Amy, clever and proud. Like a lark, she tried to escape to the clouds but always came back to nest.

Although the four sisters were very different, they loved each other so much that their strongest wish was that they would never be parted.

Times were hard. While their father was away at war, the girls and their mother struggled to make ends meet. Their house, once considered fine and elegant, had become worn and shabby. The kitchen pantry was often empty. The girls wore hand-me-down clothes. Even so, Meg, Jo, Beth, and Amy managed to have fun. Their favorite place was the cluttered attic, where any sort of make-believe seemed possible.

On Christmas eve, the girls dressed up in top hats, castoff coats, and spectacles—their Pickwick Society disguises. They sat around a table in the attic and read the latest news from their secret club's weekly newspaper, *The Pickwick Portfolio*.

Suddenly, sleigh bells jangled from the snowy street below. Jo leapt to the attic window and scanned their neighbor's yard. She was always on the lookout for new ideas for her exciting tales of danger. "What do we think of the boy next door?" Jo asked her sisters, who were busy helping themselves to their afternoon treat of tea and toast with jam. "Is he a captive? Perhaps he's being held prisoner by old Mr. Laurence."

Meg tiptoed beside Jo at the window for a better look at the mysterious young man who had just arrived in a fine carriage. He hurried up the steps of the dreary mansion, followed by servants carrying trunks and boxes. "He's had no upbringing at all, they say," Meg whispered. "He was reared in Italy among artists and vagrants."

"What's a vagrant?" demanded Amy, who was fond of eavesdropping on other people's conversations.

"Someone with no home, no money, no job, who goes wherever he pleases," Meg said in a know-it-all, eldest sister tone.

"Jehosephat!" Jo exclaimed. "Picture giving up adventures in Italy and coming to live with awful old Mr. Laurence."

"Don't say *awful*, Jo, it's slang," Meg scolded. "Mr. Laurence intends to prepare the boy for business. One day he'll inherit his grandfather's entire firm."

Jo frowned and flopped on the battered couch in the corner of the attic. "Give me the artists and vagrants."

"I shouldn't mind living in a fine house and having nice things," Meg said. She stared at the cracked teacups and sighed. "It doesn't seem like Christmas this year without presents."

"I'm desperate for good drawing pencils," said Amy, taking a sip of tea. "If I can't sketch with proper pencils, I'll never be ready to go to Rome one day and do fine pictures and be the best artist in the world."

"And you, Beth, what's your Christmas wish?" Meg asked.

"I'd like the war to end, so Father can come home," Beth replied quietly.

"Sweet Beth," Jo said. "We all want that."

From the house next door came the faint sound of music. "They do have a beautiful piano," Beth said wistfully.

"Wait till I'm a writer, I'll buy you the best piano in creation," Jo said. She sat up and ate her bread and jam in one unladylike gulp.

"And if Jo doesn't become a famous writer, Beth, you can come over and play mine," Amy promised. "When I marry, I'm going to be disgustingly rich."

"And what if the one you love is a poor man, but good, like Father?" Meg asked and smiled.

Amy stared at her reflection in her teaspoon. "It isn't like being stuck with the nose you were born with. You do have a choice about who you love. Belle Gardiner had four marriage proposals. She'll never want for nice things."

"I wouldn't marry for money," Jo said. "What if your husband's business goes bust? Look what happened to Father. Besides, down at the *Eagle* they pay five dollars for every story they print. Why, I have ten stories in my head right now!"

Meg frowned. "I don't like all this talk about money. It isn't refined."

"We'll all grow up some day, Meg," Amy replied. "We might as well know what we want."

Later that evening, the girls came downstairs to welcome their mother. Every day Marmee worked at Hope House, a place where the poor could come to get free food and clothing. "Marmee's home!"

Beth cried, carrying her mother's worn slippers that had been warmed by the fire.

The front door flew open. In stepped Marmee covered with snow. She disappeared in a tumble of hugs.

"We waited and waited. We've been expectorating you for hours," said Amy, who liked to use fancy words she often did not understand.

"*Expecting,* featherhead," Jo said and took her mother's shawl.

Marmee kissed each daughter, put on her slippers, and sat down in a chair beside the fire in the parlor. "I've a surprise for you," she said mischievously.

"A letter from Father!" Amy cried.

Marmee smiled and took the letter from her pocket. The girls listened eagerly as their mother read aloud: "My Dearest Family...I am well and safe. December makes a hard, cold season for all of us, so far from home. I pray that your own hardships will not be too great to bear. I know that the girls will remember all I said to them, that they will be loving children to you so that when I come back to them I may be fonder and prouder than ever of my little women."

The girls sniffed and wiped tears from their eyes when they heard the last words—"my little women."

"What about a song? A Christmas carol will cheer us all. Beth, will you accompany us on the piano?" Marmee asked. Beth played the old, out-of-tune piano in the parlor as best she could. Her sisters' voices blended in perfect harmony. When they finished singing, Meg, Jo, Beth, and Amy kissed Marmee good-night and went to bed.

Only Jo could not sleep. She felt restless. How would she ever make her father proud? She went upstairs to the attic. There, she put on her special velveteen writing cap and frock coat. By candle-light, she began writing another scene for her latest story, "The Lost Duke of Gloucester."

"Don't sit up late, dear," Marmee said from the attic stairs.

Jo was so busy, she did not hear her.

The next morning, Jo and her three sisters woke up and dressed as fast as they could. Christmas morning! They hurried downstairs and were surprised to find the dining room table filled with fragrant sausages, porridge, a loaf of bread, and a steaming pot of coffee.

"An absolute Christmas miracle!" Meg exclaimed. "Isn't this just like the old days, Hannah?"

Hannah nodded cheerfully. She had been the girls' housekeeper ever since they were babies.

Amy held up a precious orange to admire. "We shouldn't eat it, Hannah," Amy said solemnly, "we should just look at it."

"Jo, fetch your Marmee," Hannah said and handed Jo a cloak. "She went out early to help a poor family called the Hummels. They don't speak a word of English. Six children and a new baby on the way. Like as not they ain't got any breakfast or firewood neither."

Amy looked at the sausages and licked her lips hungrily.

Jo and her sisters exchanged glances. What should they do? "Perhaps we could send the Hummels our bread," Beth said slowly, remembering what Father had said in his letter.

"Might as well take the butter. Butter's no good without bread to put it on," Jo said. Quickly, she and her sisters gathered up the sausages, porridge, bread, coffee, and firewood and carried them down the street. As Jo marched through the snow, she kicked up her long skirts. "Wonderful snow! Don't you wish we could roll about in it like dogs?" She waved to old Mr. Laurence and his mysterious grandson who stood on the porch dressed for church. "Lovely weather for a picnic!" she called.

"Jo!" Meg said angrily. "What will they think of us?"

Amy, Beth, and Jo only laughed and hurried on. "Merry Christmas!" the girls cried when they reached the shack in the alley.

The door opened. When Jo and her sisters looked inside, they were shocked to see three small, dirty children on a bed, shivering beneath one blanket. With them lay their mother, whose face was pale and damp. Marmee motioned for the girls to come inside. In her arms, she held a tiny, wrinkled newborn swaddled in rags. "Stoke up the fire, my little women," she said gently. The four girls filled the small stove with fresh wood and shared their Christmas breakfast with the hungry children.

CHAPTER TWO

New Year's Day

On New Year's Day, Jo and Meg received an invitation to a party at Belle Gardiner's. Amy, who considered herself an authority on social events, ran around the house searching for proper handkerchiefs and hair ribbons. She dug through boxes of castoff clothing for Meg and discovered high-heeled silk boots that were too tight but perfectly charming. Downstairs in the kitchen, Beth scrubbed Jo's stained gloves and patched her skirt, which had scorched when she stood too close to the fire.

"Hold still," said Jo, who claimed to know how to create the latest hairdo. When she unwound Meg's hair from the red-hot curling iron, a handful of scorched friz fell to the floor.

"You've ruined me!" Meg screamed. "I can't go like this!"

"Good," said Jo, who never liked fancy dress-up dances. "I'm not going either."

"I'll never have any suitors." Meg moaned. "I'll just die an old maid."

"Here, we'll tie a bow in front," Amy said helpfully, arranging Meg's hair with her own ribbon. "You don't need lots of suitors. You only need one if he's the right one."

"Meg isn't going to be married right away, is she?" Beth asked worriedly.

"She's never getting married," Jo said with authority.

"With your help, I never will!" Meg replied. "Jo, mind you don't eat much supper. Don't say 'Jehosephat,' and don't shake hands with people. Don't forget to keep your back to the wall so no one can see the patch on your skirt."

The girls said good-bye to Marmee. As they walked down the sidewalk, Jo wondered how she'd ever be able to remember so many "don'ts." Her brain felt as if it had been pierced by all nineteen of her hairpins.

Meg wasn't the least bit nervous. "I have a wonderful feeling about tonight," she told Jo and glided gracefully up the steps into the Gardiner's elegant home.

While Meg whirled away in a waltz, Jo groped along the edge of the room with her back to the wall. She had to escape. What if someone asked her to dance? As fast as she could, she bolted behind some curtains.

Crash!

Jo fell head over heels into the mysterious captive from next door. "Jehosephat!" she exclaimed. "I'm sorry. I didn't know someone else was hiding here."

"Don't go!" said the handsome young man, who appeared to be eighteen years old. He took another bite of his dish of ice cream. "I just came here so I could stare at people. I'm Theodore Laurence, but I'm called Laurie."

Jo put out her hand, then remembered Meg's advice and tucked her hand behind her. "I'm Jo March. Who were you staring at?"

"I'm quite taken with that one," Laurie said, peering and pointing through the curtains.

"That's Meg, my sister. She's completely bald in front," Jo said. Pleased to have shocked Laurie, she took a quick sample of his melting ice cream. "Do you speak French or Italian?"

"English at home. French at school."

"What school?"

"The Conservatory of Music in Vevey," Laurie said and then added unhappily, "Since I've come to live with Grandfather, he's having me tutored. He insists I go to college here in America."

"Where are your parents?"

"Europe."

"I wish I could go to college," Jo said wistfully, then smiled at Laurie. "Of course, if I weren't going to be a famous writer, I'd go to New York and become an actress. Are you shocked?"

"Very," Laurie said, grinning. "Would you like to dance?"

"Can't," Jo whispered. "I burned my dress in back."

"That's too bad. But no one will notice if we dance in the hall. Come on," Laurie said, beckoning her out from behind the curtain.

She joined him in a wild, silly polka. "Are you looking at my dress? You promised not to, you cheat!" Jo said. She laughed as they twirled and stomped down the hallway.

Their polka ended abruptly when they stumbled into Meg. She sat on the back stairs holding one of her high-heeled boots. "Jo, I've sprained my ankle," she said and sobbed.

"I shouldn't wonder in those shoes," Laurie said.

Meg sniffed loudly. She frowned at Laurie.

"This is our neighbor, Meg. He's the captive," said Jo.

"A perfectly good party ruined," muttered Meg, paying no attention to her sister's introduction. "How will we get home?"

"Allow me," said Laurie, and he made a little bow. True to his

word, he took the girls home in his grandfather's carriage. "Good night, Mrs. March," he said politely at the door.

"You two have all the luck!" exclaimed Amy, who was hiding on the stairway in her nightgown. "Oh, Jo, is he very romantic?"

Jo frowned. "Not in the slightest."

"He's a dreadful boy," Meg said, wincing as Marmee examined the sprain.

"He put ice on your ankle with his own hands?" Amy asked.

"Oh, stop being swoony," Jo said. "You mustn't be soppy about Laurie, any more than you'd be soppy about a dog or a chair. I hope we shall be friends with him."

"With a boy?" Amy asked in disbelief.

"He isn't a boy," Jo replied. "He's Laurie."

CHAPTER THREE

Work Days, School Days, and Pickled Limes

In the weeks that followed, Laurie visited Jo and her sisters nearly every day. They threw snowballs, zoomed downhill on sleds, and built fat snowmen. Their hours together always disappeared quickly. Soon the fun ended, and it was time to go to work or school again.

To earn money, Jo went to Aunt March's house and kept her cranky old relative company. Meg made a few dollars each week caring for two young children. Amy attended school. Only Beth, who was too shy to go anywhere, stayed home and made herself useful by cleaning, cooking, and caring for Mrs. Pat-Paw's growing brood of kittens.

"Blast these wretched skirts!" Jo exclaimed early one morning as she trudged through the snow with Meg and Amy.

"Don't say 'blast' and 'wretch,'" Amy scolded.

"I like good strong words," Jo replied.

Amy stumbled and dropped her slate with her homework into a puddle. She groaned. "Why do I have to go to school? I'm so degenerated I can hardly hold my head up. I owe at least a dozen limes."

"Are limes the fashion now?" Meg asked.

Amy nodded woefully. "Everyone keeps them in their desks and trades them for beads and things. All the girls treat each other at recess. If you don't bring limes to school, you're nothing. I've had ever so many, and I can't pay anyone back."

"No wonder you never learn anything at that school," Jo said with disgust.

"Here's a quarter," Meg said, handing Amy some of Marmee's rag money. "I know how it feels to do without any little luxuries."

Amy threw her arms around Meg, delighted that she could buy limes and be just like all the other girls. She hurried the rest of the way to Mr. Davis's School for Young Ladies. "Oh, have you limes, Amy dear?" whispered one of the girls in the cloakroom.

"I'll treat you at noon," Amy said proudly.

"How ever did you get limes?" asked May Chester, the teacher's pet. "Were they donated to Hope House?"

Amy whirled and replied, "You'll not get a single pickled lime from me, May Chester."

"Young ladies, your slates, please," Mr. Davis announced and rapped the floor with his long, wooden pointer. Amy gulped and slipped the packet of limes inside her desk.

"Excuse me, Mr. Davis?" said May Chester. "Did you not forbid us to indulge in limes?"

"I will not have this distracting fad in my school," Mr. Davis said.

May Chester smiled. "Miss March is hiding a whole packet."

Mr. Davis yanked open the lid of Amy's desk, grabbed the precious limes, and threw them out the window. "Put out your hand," he told Amy. She raised her hand. Down came the pointer. Whack!

After school ended, Amy ran to Aunt March's to tell Jo how she

had been punished. "Mr. Davis ought to be arrested at once!" Jo said angrily. "And if not arrested, then strangled!"

When Marmee came home from work that evening and saw the welt on Amy's hand, she wrote a letter withdrawing her from the school. "Jo can help you with your lessons," Marmee said as she tucked Amy in bed. "Will you discipline yourself to study at home?"

Amy nodded uncertainly and sighed. "I'm perfectly desolated when I think of all those lovely limes."

"I am not sorry you lost them, if it will help you govern your vanities," Marmee said. "You have a good many little gifts and virtues, but there is no need parading them any more than you would dress up in all your gowns, bonnets, and ribbons all at once, to show folks you have them." Then she kissed each daughter good-night.

Later that evening, Jo slipped up into the attic to write. "Is it a good story?" Beth asked, tiptoeing behind her.

"Don't know. It's all murder and gore," Jo replied and showed her sister what she had written. "Beth, truly, I don't think I'll ever be like Marmee. I rather crave violence. If only I could go to war like Father and right wrongs."

"And so Marmee does, in her own way."

"I want to do something splendid," Jo said quietly. "Something that turns the world upside down."

Beth smiled. "Perhaps you will."

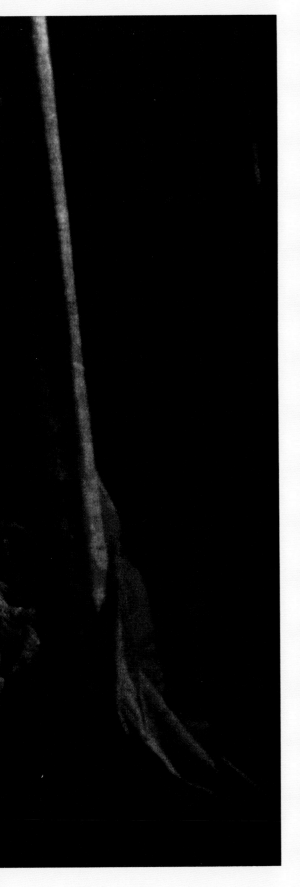

CHAPTER FOUR

Sharing Secrets

A few weeks later on a dreary winter day, Laurie opened his window and called, "Hello, come over, Jo! It's dull as tombs around here." He waved to Jo and Meg, who were carrying firewood indoors.

John Brooke, Laurie's tutor, yanked Laurie back inside. "Mr. Laurence, one doesn't shout at ladies as if they were cattle!" Mr. Brooke scolded. "To your work, sir!" He nodded to Jo and Meg and closed the window, lingering just a moment to watch lovely Meg.

Unlike Laurie, Jo and her sisters were free to do as they pleased when they finished their day's work and chores around the house. One of the girls' favorite things to do was to perform plays that Jo wrote. Their theater was in the attic, where they piled chairs and tables to make scenery and rigged a stage curtain with a rope and an old bedsheet.

Later that afternoon, Jo and her sisters rehearsed their latest production.

"Oh dear Countess, pray for me!" wailed Meg, dressed in a lavender shawl as Lady Violet.

"Say 'sinned' as if you really mean it," shouted Jo, director, stage manager, and Duke. She sported a beard of smeared soot and a gleaming helmet that was once a cooking pot.

"I want to be Lady Violet," whined Amy, who was dressed in tights and an oversized coat as Rodrigo. "I'm exhaustified of being the boy."

"Here, be the Countess de Montascu," Beth said. She offered Amy her baby. The wriggling, furry infant was Mrs. Pat-Paw, their cat, dressed up in a piece of flannel and a small bonnet.

"The Countess doesn't have any lines," Amy complained.

Meg sighed impatiently and handed Amy Rodrigo's hat. "Well, who's going to play Rodrigo?"

Jo rapped her wooden sword on the floor. "Gentlemen, I propose the admission of a new actor to our theater. Theodore Laurence."

Amy, Beth, and Meg looked at each other in shock. "He'll laugh at our acting and make fun of us," Amy protested.

"He'll think it's only a game," Beth agreed.

"He won't, upon my word as a gentleman," Jo said. "Oh please, let's try him, shall we?"

The attic closet door flew open. Out jumped Laurie, grinning. Amy, Meg, and Beth screamed and dove behind the castle scenery to hide. "Jo, how could you?" they shrieked. Mrs. Pat-Paw tore off her bonnet and streaked downstairs.

"Fellow artists," Laurie announced and bowed, "may I present myself as an actor, musician, and loyal and *very* humble servant of the Pickwick Society. To show you how grateful I am and to promote communication of secrets, I shall provide a post office in our hedge." He took a birdhouse with a hinged roof from the closet to show the girls. "I do pledge never to reveal what I receive in confidence here."

Jo and her sisters cheered. Meg handed Laurie a copy of the script. "Take your place, Rodrigo," she told him. With a flourish, Laurie placed Rodrigo's plumed hat on his head.

CHAPTER FIVE

Going to a Play

Early one morning in late winter, Jo went into the woods not far from her house. She listened to the sound of the old trees swaying in the wind. Kneeling on the prickly bed of pine needles, she loosened her bootlaces. Then she tied her jacket around her waist and unfastened her beautiful long hair. Off she sprinted through the trees, gracefully hurdling a frozen stream.

When she arrived breathlessly back at home, she opened the post office birdhouse roof and shouted with delight, "Four theater tickets for tonight!" She read the note from Laurie and ran inside to tell her sisters and Marmee. She and Meg were going to the theater with Laurie and Mr. Brooke!

"I want to go, too," Amy said when she heard the news. "I never go anywhere."

Jo paid no attention to her pouting

youngest sister. "You're too little. Beth, where is Marmee's opera glass?"

"I'm not little," insisted Amy, who did not like to be reminded that she was the youngest in the family. "You're just hogging Laurie. Please, can I go?"

"There are only four tickets," Meg replied as she came downstairs in her best dress.

"You're weeks behind in your schoolwork. Finish the pages I've marked," Jo said. "And don't sulk. You look like a pigeon."

Amy scowled. A carriage arrived at the door. Jo and Meg hurried outside. When the door slammed, Amy bellowed, "You'll be sorry for this, Jo March!"

The play that evening was just as delightful as Jo had imagined it would be. Her only disappointment was the strange way Meg acted all the way home. What was wrong with her? Meg cooed as coyly as a silly, lovesick parakeet.

Disgusted, Jo decided to teach her sister a lesson. She nudged Mr. Brooke with her elbow and said loudly, "The star of the play certainly swooned wonderfully, don't you think? Meg is a sensational actress, too. We're always putting on wild theatricals."

Meg blushed. "It's just something we play at," she said, horrified. When she resumed her composure, she offered Mr. Brooke her hand. But Jo was too quick. She pushed Meg through the gate and up the front steps.

"Thank you very much and good night!" Jo shouted.

When the girls came in the front door, Meg turned on Jo in fury. "That was rude."

"You plastered yourself on him!" Jo replied.

"It's proper to take a gentleman's arm if it's offered," Meg said.

Marmee looked up at the girls from her desk in the parlor. "How was the play?" she asked.

"Wonderful, I was absolutely inspired by the love scene," Jo replied and made a face at Meg. Meg blushed and fled into the kitchen.

Jo kissed her mother good-night and got ready for bed. She poked her head in Amy's room. "Still sulking?" she asked.

Amy lay in bed, pretending to read a book. She did not answer, but glanced nervously at the fire burning brightly in the small grate in her bedroom.

"Well, good-night," Jo said. She went into the room she shared with Beth and began searching for the manuscript she was working on. Where was it?

"Beth," Jo whispered, "have you seen my manuscript?"

Beth snored, fast asleep. Jo paused and looked around. Slowly, her face filled with horror. She rushed into Amy and Meg's room and knelt at the fireplace. There she watched in disbelief as "The Lost Duke of Gloucester" burned and crumbled into ash.

"I hate you as long as I live!" Jo screamed and jumped on Amy's bed.

"I didn't do it!" Amy shrieked.

Jo shook and slapped Amy in a wild rage. Marmee and Meg rushed upstairs and pulled the girls apart as Jo gave one last kick, shouting, "You're not my sister. You're nothing. You're dead!"

Marmee managed to drag Jo back to her own room. Jo flopped on her bed, sobbing.

"Jo, it's a great loss," Marmee said. "You've every right to be put out. But don't let the sun go down upon your anger. Forgive each other and begin again tomorrow."

Jo shook her head furiously. She clenched her fist and kept her face to the wall. "I'll never forgive Amy," Jo said hoarsely.

Amy, lingering in the doorway, sadly turned away and returned to her own room.

Thin Ice

The next day, Jo still felt angry at Amy. She decided to escape from her house and her sister by going skating with Laurie. Didn't she deserve to have some fun after what Amy had done to her? She told herself that this might be her last chance to skate on the pond before spring came and melted what was left of the ice.

"Watch out here, it's weak!" she called to Laurie.

The blades of his skates flashed in the sunlight. He tossed a stick on the ice to mark the spot where the ice was melting. "And careful here!" he said.

"Race you to the mark!" Jo said. She pointed to the tree that always marked the finish line.

"You say go," Laurie said and grinned.

In the distance a voice called, "Laurie! Jo! Wait for me!"

Jo looked over her shoulder. She recognized Amy's red-and-white cap and let out a great mouthful of air in disgust. "Ignore her. Ready? Go!" She and Laurie streaked to the other side of the pond.

Amy stumbled along the shore waving a mitten. "No fair!" she said to herself. She fumbled with the laces of her ice skates and skated awkwardly toward her sister.

Crack! The ice buckled and gave way. Amy was swallowed in suffocating cold. She tried to scream. Water filled her nose, her mouth. She tried to wave her arms. Her skates tangled in her long skirt. Weights seemed to pull her deeper, deeper.

When Jo heard the ice split, she turned. At that instant, all she could spot was her sister's red-and-white hat floating in the gaping patch of dark water. "Amy!" Jo yelled. Her legs seemed frozen to the spot. Something dark sped past.

"Bring me a stick, a rail—anything!" shouted Laurie. He dashed to the hole in the ice. Quickly, he dropped to his knees and then to his stomach and reached. But his arms weren't long enough to catch hold of Amy.

Jo sped to the shore and tore a rail from a fence around the pond. She threw it. Ice cracked beneath her feet. Following Laurie's example, she lay flat on her stomach and slithered out to the hole.

"Hold on, Amy!" Laurie shouted and held out the rail. Amy's hand surfaced. She made a grab, missed, and slipped away.

"Do something!" Jo screamed.

Laurie tried again, this time with help from Jo. Together they caught Amy's arms. They dragged her gasping out of the water. Inch by inch, they hauled her to solid ice closer to shore.

Laurie struggled out of his coat and wrapped Amy in it. Her teeth chattered. "Can't f-f-feel my legs," Amy stammered between bluish lips.

Jo stripped off her own wool skirt, leaving only her bloomers. She used the skirt to wrap around her sister's legs. "We've got to get her home fast," Laurie said. He tore away the laces of his skates and

picked Amy up in his arms. He and Jo dashed through the woods.

When they arrived at home, Marmee went to work bundling Amy in blankets beside the kitchen fire. Soon she was covered with comforters, shawls, and several hot water bottles. For good measure, four warm kittens lay curled and mewing in her lap.

"Josephine March, I can't believe you walked all the way home in only your bloomers!" Meg said as she hung Jo and Amy's damp clothes in front of the fire to dry.

Jo did not pay any attention to Meg. She was too worried about Amy. "I'm sorry I'm so horrible," she whispered to her sister.

"No, I'm sorry," Amy said in a low voice. "I'm much more horribler than you."

"What if you'd drowned? What if Laurie hadn't been there?" Jo said. She gave Amy a hug.

"Jo, do you love Laurie more than you love me?"

Jo chuckled. "Don't be such a beetle. I'll never love anyone as I love my sisters."

Amy slipped her hand into Jo's. Jo squeezed it tightly. That evening, the two girls sat on the bed and tried to recall the lost manuscript. Jo hunched over the paper and wrote rapidly.

"No, no, we're leaving out the best part," Amy said. "Right, yes, the grotto scene," Jo said and scribbled faster.

"I adore the grotto scene," Amy said. She and Jo were so busy rewriting "The Lost Duke of Gloucester," they did not notice Marmee standing in the doorway, watching them and smiling.

CHAPTER SEVEN

Spring 1863—
to the Ball

On a lovely spring day, Meg hastily packed her new pale blue dress in a suitcase. That very afternoon she was to travel to Boston with Aunt March and her dreadful poodle. The trip was her aunt's idea. "How is Meg to be married without a proper debut?" Aunt March had told Marmee. She planned for Meg to attend all kinds of dances and parties—the perfect place to find a rich husband.

Of course Meg was thrilled. She waved farewell to her sisters and climbed into the carriage. Nothing could have prepared her, however, for the finery she discovered when they arrived at the home of Miss Sally Moffat in Boston. Meg had never seen such a magnificent house!

On the afternoon before the big ball, Meg joined a chatty group of young ladies her age. They gathered upstairs to admire Belle Gardiner's enormous engagement ring. When it was time to get ready, the girls inspected each other's dresses.

"Oh, Meg, I do like that color on you!" Sally Moffat exclaimed when she saw Meg's new dress.

"It's a wonderful blue," agreed beautiful Belle Gardiner. "The nicest cotton I've seen since the war broke out. But you had it made up so plain."

"Well, I-I-I do my own sewing and—" Meg stammered.

Belle laughed. "Mrs. Finster's on Charles Street carries silk pieces ready-made. Tomorrow I'll take you there." She kissed Meg on the cheek and promised to lend her one of her own ball gowns. "I'm going to make you my pet. Tonight Miss March shall have as many conquests as she likes."

The most important people in society attended the ball that night. Gentlemen arrived in fine waistcoats and top hats. Ladies wore elegant gowns and jewels. The Moffat ballroom echoed with laughter and music.

When Meg walked down the steps in Belle's apricot-yellow gown, everyone turned to look at her. Bracelets covered her arms. Pearls circled her neck. She had been powdered and squeezed and made to look exactly like the most fashionable women from Paris. Her lips and cheeks were colored with rouge; her hair was curled about her head. In her new outfit, jewelry, and hairdo, she felt as if she'd become someone new—someone bold and powerful and dangerously beautiful.

With a haughty sneer, Meg smiled at the eager young men gathered around her. She took a sip of champagne offered to her on a tray.

"Miss March?" a voice interrupted.

Meg looked up and nearly choked. Standing in front of her was Laurie. His arms were crossed, and he was frowning.

"I want to report everything I see here to Jo," he said.

Horrified, Meg blushed and ran from the ballroom.

Laurie followed her. "I'm sorry," he said.

"Please don't tell Jo how I look or how I've behaved," Meg said and began to cry. "I was just playing a part—to see how it felt to be Belle Gardiner with four proposals and twenty pairs of gloves."

"Why not just be who you really are?" Laurie asked. He handed her a handkerchief. "You're worth ten of those other girls."

Meg tried to smile. As best she could, she wiped Belle's bright rouge from her mouth.

CHAPTER EIGHT

Autumn 1864

Months passed. The leaves changed color, and soon it was fall again. Laurie, now nineteen years old, finished his studies with Mr. Brooke and prepared to leave for college. Jo helped him pack his books. "I'm sure you'll come home so brilliant," Jo said, "you'll find me impossible to talk to. I'll be so utterly dull."

Laurie stared hard at Jo. "Nothing's going to change."

"I wish I could go to college," Jo admitted.

"I wish you could too."

Jo smiled mischievously. "You'll learn all sorts of things I don't know, and then I'll hate you."

"Oh?" Laurie said and raised one eyebrow. "I already know something you don't know. It's about Meg and a certain former tutor of mine."

"Liar," Jo said hotly.

"Has Meg mislaid a certain personal article?" Laurie said and smiled. "Such as a glove?"

Jo tried to pretend she wasn't interested in Laurie's secret. But she thought about what he had told her on her way home. When she came into the kitchen, she discovered Hannah and Meg making biscuits. "Meg, John Brooke stole your glove!" Jo announced. "Laurie says he keeps it in his pocket."

Meg turned bright red and looked pleased. This only made Jo more upset. "You must tell him to return it," Jo insisted. "I'm going to tell Marmee." As she turned to leave the kitchen, Marmee appeared in the doorway. She held a telegram in her shaking hand.

"What is it?" Jo asked.

"It's from the Washington Hotel Hospital," Marmee said, her face pale. "Your father has been wounded. I must go to him at once."

Jo and her sisters felt shocked and frightened. What if Father died? They tried to comfort their mother and helped her pack for the long trip. Mr. Brooke offered to accompany Marmee. Mr. Laurence ordered his cook to pack a supper and bottles of medicine for Father.

As the time grew closer for Marmee to leave, Amy paced the parlor nervously. "Where is Jo? It's almost seven. The train will be leaving soon," Amy said. Meg and Beth carried Marmee's suitcase and basket to the door.

"She's gone to Aunt March's to get money for a railway ticket," Meg replied. "She should be back by now. What could be keeping her?"

Marmee looked up from the desk where she was writing last-minute notes. The front door slammed. In rushed Jo in her bonnet and coat. Her cheeks were flushed, and she had a strange expression on her face as she placed a fistful of money on Marmee's desk.

"Twenty-five dollars?" Marmee said, counting out the bills. "Can Aunt March spare it?"

Jo shook her head. "I couldn't bear to ask her. I sold my hair instead." Dramatically, she swept off her bonnet and revealed her short, ragged hairdo. "I was walking by the barbershop and saw a long bunch of hair hanging in the window. A sign said twenty-five dollars. So I had my hair cut and sold it." Jo laughed nervously.

Her sisters gathered around her, speechless. "How could you?" Amy asked. "Your hair was your one beauty."

Jo ran her hand through her stubby locks and said as bravely as she could, "It'll grow back."

Marmee, with tears in her eyes, rose from her chair. She hugged Jo. "I shall miss my little women," she whispered. Then she kissed each daughter. "Don't forget to go and take care of the Hummels every day while I am gone."

"Tell Father we love him," Meg said.

"Tell him we pray for him," Beth added.

Amy blew her nose in a handkerchief. "Bring him home."

The girls and Hannah waved good-bye. They stood at the window and watched the Laurence carriage disappear as Marmee was driven to the train station.

That night, the four sisters slept uneasily. With both their mother and father gone, it seemed to them as if their whole world had fallen apart. Beth sat up and looked about the bedroom. What was that strange noise? She glanced at Jo's bed and in the moonlight saw that it was empty. Across the room, she could see the outline of her sister sitting on an old chair, weeping.

"Are you thinking of Father?" Beth whispered. She got out of bed and put her arm around Jo.

Jo shook her head. With heartfelt misery, she cried, "My hair!" Beth hugged her. They both began to cry and laugh at the same time.

CHAPTER NINE

On Their Own

Jo and her sisters tried their best to keep the house running smoothly while their mother was gone. But the job was bigger and more daunting than they realized. Cooking, cleaning, and mending never seemed to end. Meg and Jo kept track of their dwindling money. Beth and Amy took turns making breakfast and dinner.

"Oh, dear! This stove!" Amy cried. She stabbed a crispy black potato with a fork. It rolled and splintered onto the floor.

"There's no cornmeal or coffee. The grocer won't let us have more on our account," Meg said sadly, inspecting the pantry. "What can I bring the Hummels to eat?" Beth asked.

"Oh, fry the Hummels!" Jo exclaimed. "You spent hours there last week. We'll be late, Meg. Put a potato in your pocket. At least it will keep your hands warm."

While Jo and Meg hurried off to

work, Beth took her blackened potato to the Hummels. When she knocked at their door, she was surprised when Mrs. Hummel answered and began yelling at her in German. Around her skirts clung the other children. Their lips were cracked, their eyes looked feverish. The baby squalled loudly. What should she do, Beth wondered? Uncertainly, she took the baby and followed Mrs. Hummel inside.

While Beth spent the day struggling to care for the sick Hummel children, Jo read aloud to Aunt March until she dozed off in her chair. When it was finally time to go home, Jo rushed out the door. She raced up her front steps two at a time and checked the mailbox.

"Jehosephat!" she exclaimed. She rushed into the parlor. "Meg! Beth! You won't believe it. I just sold 'The Lost Duke of Gloucester.' They sent me five whole dollars. I'm an author! Wait till I tell Laurie. I noticed he's home from college and—" Jo stopped. "What's wrong, Beth?"

Her sister sat slumped at the old piano. When she looked up at Jo, her eyes were red as if from weeping. "The Hummel baby died in my arms," Beth said in a sad, tired voice. "I feel so very strange."

Jo frantically called Meg and Amy. Together they managed to help Beth upstairs and put her to bed. "She's burning up, but she says she's freezing," Meg whispered to her sisters. "She has a terrible thirst, but she won't drink. What should we do?"

When Hannah arrived, she brought terrible news. "I seen the Hummels," she said. "Two children taken up to Jesus. Scarlet fever. Meg and Miss Jo won't be harmed, you had it when you were babies. But Miss Amy we have to send away to stay with Aunt March."

Amy did not want to be sent away. But there was no choice. Laurie volunteered to take Amy in his carriage across town to Aunt March's so that she might be spared catching the dread disease.

"I don't want to go," Amy said as the carriage rolled and lurched down the street. "I'm afraid of Aunt March."

"If she's unkind to you, I'll come and take you away," Laurie promised.

"Where will we go?" Amy demanded.

"Paris," Laurie replied and smiled.

Amy laughed and then suddenly grew serious. "If I get scarlet fever and die, give Meg my box with the green doves. Jo must have my turquoise ring."

"I'll see to it."

Amy sniffed. "I don't want to die. I've never even been kissed. I've waited my whole life to be kissed, and what if I miss it?"

Laurie tried to keep a straight face. "Tell you what. I promise to kiss you before you die."

Amy grinned. When the carriage hit a bump, she gave him a hug and secretly kissed his coat sleeve.

That evening Beth's fever grew worse. Jo and her sister Meg tried their best to make her comfortable. But nothing they did seemed to help. "Beth needs Marmee," Jo whispered to Meg. "She depends on her."

"What if we send for Marmee," Meg said, "and Father gets worse?"

"And how would we pay for the train?" Hannah asked.

When Dr. Bangs came to check Beth, the news was not good. "There's nothing more that can be done," he said in a low voice to Jo and Meg. "It's best to send for your mother."

Jo dropped into a chair, numb. It might be days before Marmee received word and caught the train home. By then it might be too late.

"Forgive me," Laurie said. "I have already sent a telegram. Mrs. March arrives on the late train tonight."

Jo was so happy when she heard this, she jumped up and hugged Laurie—much to his astonishment.

Just as Laurie promised, Marmee arrived that evening. She went to work to bring Beth's fever under control.

All night, Marmee, Jo, and Meg bathed Beth's face with water. Jo was so tired, she fell asleep in a chair outside her sister's room.

Suddenly, Jo awoke with a start. She heard Hannah sobbing. Jo jumped to her feet. What had happened? She pushed open Beth's door, filled with dread.

Her sister opened her eyes. She smiled weakly at Jo. Jo ran to her and knelt beside her bed. With a thin little hand, Beth stroked Jo's short curls.

CHAPTER TEN

Christmas Eve 1864

On Christmas eve, Marmee, Jo, and her sisters gathered in the parlor. They were joined by Laurie, his grandfather Mr. Laurence, and Aunt March. Fragrant evergreen bows decorated the entrance way. Beth played carols on the lovely new rosewood piano Mr. Laurence had given her as a gift. In spite of the warm feeling in the room, the holiday was missing someone important. For the second Christmas in a row, Father was still gone away to war.

Jo slipped into the kitchen to get coffee for their guests. As she opened the door, she heard Marmee say, "Meg, I fear you would have a very long engagement. Three years, or four. John must do his military service before he can marry, and he has much to secure. He has no house. His position is uncertain—"

"You call him 'John'?" Jo interrupted. "Don't you mean 'Mr. Brooke'?"

"Jo!" Meg said, looking startled.

"Well, he is there at Washington Hospital with Father every day," Marmee said.

"That conniving rook!" Jo replied indignantly. "Sneaking around currying up to Father and you to steal our Meg and carry her off. I won't let him have you." She paused and looked pleadingly at Marmee. "We don't have to get married, do we?"

Marmee sighed. "Better never to be married than be unhappy."

Meg's face reddened. "Do you think I'd be unhappy married to John?"

"Poky old Brooke?" Jo said and laughed harshly. "He's dull as powder and poor besides."

Marmee frowned. "I'd rather Meg be a poor man's wife and well loved than marry for riches and lose her self-respect."

Meg's face brightened. "Then you don't mind that John Brooke is poor?"

"You're not going to let her get married, are you?" Jo pleaded.

"It's a proposal, nothing more. It needn't be decided right now," Marmee said hurriedly. "I should like John to be established in a good business first."

With delight, Meg gave Marmee a hug. Jo pouted as she pushed open the kitchen door. Coming from the hallway, she heard voices and wondered what new guests had just arrived. She hurried to see. To her amazement, she saw two familiar figures. One was John Brooke. The other was Father, still wearing his army uniform. His arm hung in a sling at his side.

Overjoyed to see him safe and well, Jo and her sisters rushed to hug him. "What a Christmas present!" Amy cried.

"You grew your beard," Meg said.

"You look handsome!" Beth replied.

Aunt March came close for a better look. She wrinkled up her nose. "He's very puny."

The girls laughed and led Father to the sofa. "I'm not used to this much attention," he said. "Don't coddle this soldier too much."

"Meg, take his cloak," Marmee ordered, bustling about the room. She handed Father's muddy boots to Jo. "Take these outside and give them a good shake."

Jo hurried to do as she was told. But when she opened the door, she could hardly believe her eyes. Meg and John Brooke were kissing in the snowy doorway.

CHAPTER ELEVEN

Spring 1867

Two years passed. Two more Christmas holidays came and went. The war finally ended. Jo, now twenty-one years old, struggled to act like a proper lady even though she still enjoyed jumping fences. Beth, eighteen, remained pale and frail. Sixteen-year-old Amy had blossomed into a lovely young woman.

Of all four sisters, the one who had changed the most was Meg, twenty-two. One lovely spring afternoon, she married John Brooke in the garden, surrounded by family and friends. Meg looked beautiful in her simple dress and flowers in her hair. Although she was not marrying a rich man and would not live in a grand house, Meg's face glowed with happiness.

Jo watched the guests hurry to congratulate Meg and John Brooke. She felt strangely sad knowing that she and her sisters would never be together—telling secrets, performing plays—the way that had once been so long ago. Beth gave Jo an encouraging smile. Even so, Jo could not rid herself of a feeling of gloom. Why did everyone have to grow up? Why did everything have to change?

Jo left the wedding party and wandered along her favorite path in the woods. She was surprised to discover that Laurie had followed her. Finished with college now, he was twenty-two, handsome, and quite pleased with himself.

He hurried to catch up with Jo. "I have something to tell you."

"Speak," said Jo playfully.

Laurie cleared his throat nervously. "I have loved you since the moment I clapped eyes on you. What could be more reasonable than to marry you?"

Jo looked shocked and turned away. "We'd kill each other."

"Nonsense."

"Neither of us can keep our temper."

"I can," he said and chuckled, "unless provoked."

"We're both stupidly stubborn, especially you. We'd only quarrel—"

"I wouldn't!"

"You see, you can't even propose without quarreling!"

Laurie laughed and drew Jo closer. "Jo, dear Jo, I swear I'd be a saint. I'd let you win every argument. And I'd take care of you, and your family, and give you every luxury you've ever been denied. And you won't have to scribble at your little stories."

Jo looked at him, insulted. "I don't want to stop writing."

"And why should you, if it makes you happy?" he continued hurriedly. "Grandfather will give us his house in London. He wants me to learn the business there. Can't you see us bashing around London? You'll hardly have time to write."

Jo sighed. "Oh, Laurie, I'm not fashionable enough for London. You need someone elegant and refined."

"I want you."

Jo turned away again. "Please don't ask me. I'm so desperately

sorry. I do care for you with all my heart. But I can't go and be a wife. It's everything I never wanted."

Laurie's face darkened with anger. "You say you won't, but you will. There'll come a time when you'll meet some man, a good man, and you'll love him tremendously and live and die for him. You will, I know you! And I'll be hanged if I stand by and watch."

Laurie stalked away and did not stop to look back. Saddened and shaken, Jo stumbled down the path toward home. As she passed the hedge between her house and Laurie's, she took one last guilty look. The birdhouse post office was gone—torn from the hedge.

That evening after dinner, Jo disappeared into the attic. Tearfully, she began packing her books into boxes. Amy and Beth followed her upstairs, sensing something was wrong.

"You refused to marry Laurie?" Amy said in shock. "I'm sure you can take it back. It's just a misunderstanding."

"No," Jo said firmly and wiped her eyes.

Amy gave Beth a confused look and shrugged her shoulders.

"You're really leaving?" Amy said slowly.

"I must get away," Jo continued.

Amy put her finger to her mouth and thought for a moment. "Aunt March is going to France—"

"France!" Jo's face brightened. "That's ideal."

"But, Jo—" Amy interrupted.

"Oh, I'd put up with anything—"

Amy took a deep breath. "Aunt March has asked me to go."

Jo stared at her sister in disbelief. "To Europe? My Europe?"

"Well, I am Aunt March's companion now," Amy said proudly. "It's a good opportunity. I'm to study painting. And Aunt March hopes, with a little polish, that I shall make a good match abroad."

Jo did not reply. She felt too sad, too disappointed. That evening when Marmee came into her room to say good-night, Jo began to cry. She sobbed with her face buried in Marmee's lap.

"It isn't easy for little birds to leave the nest," Marmee said gently, stroking Jo's hair. "And just as hard for me to let you go. Amy found a way to try her wings. And now you must too, though I don't know what I'll do without my Jo."

Jo looked up. Marmee kissed her worried forehead.

"I pray you'll find your happiness," Marmee continued. "Go and have your liberty and see what comes of it."

CHAPTER TWELVE

Jo Tries Her Wings

Jo traveled alone by train to New York. The city was much bigger than she had imagined. She held tight to her carpetbags and stumbled along, trying to find her way along the crowded streets. A horse-drawn trolley clattered past at high speed. Ragged children shouted to passers-by, "Kindling! Kindling for sale!" Soot, wood smoke, and dust filled her nose and stung her eyes. Which way should she go? She walked on and on, feeling lost, tired, and hungry.

She peered at the scrap of paper in her hand and compared it with the address on a large, brown, stone building. Taking a deep breath, she climbed the long flight of steps and knocked at the door. "You must be Jo March," greeted a kindly woman. Behind her hid two little girls. "I'm Mrs. Kirke. These are my two daughters, Kitty and Minnie. You will be their tutor and governess. Please come in."

Kitty and Minnie giggled and followed

Jo as Mrs. Kirke showed her to her room. It was located on the top floor and was just big enough for a bed, a table, a chair, and a small stove. "You'll take your meals downstairs in the dining room," Mrs. Kirke said. "All my guests are of the best quality. I think you'll find I keep a very respectable boardinghouse."

In the weeks that followed, Minnie and Kitty kept Jo very busy with their lessons and trips to the park. Late at night, Jo wrote exciting stories. One day, she decided to be brave and take some of her work to the office of *The Weekly Volcano*, a newspaper.

The editor puffed his cigar. "Our subscribers are not interested in sentiment and fairy stories, Miss," he said gruffly.

Jo frowned. "It isn't a fairy story."

"Try one of the ladies' magazines," he replied.

Jo took the folder filled with her work and stomped angrily down the steps. She was in such a hurry, she did not watch where she was going and crashed into someone with a big, battered, black umbrella on the steps outside Mrs. Kirke's house. Jo's folder tumbled. Pages blew into the street.

"Oh, I'm very sorry, I'm so clumsy," said the man with the umbrella. His voice was deep, and he spoke with a German accent. Jo darted out into the street to snatch a page tumbling in the wind. A wagon rolled closer. Jo reached. Just in time, she felt herself jerked backward. The wagon wheel whizzed past. Thanks to the man with the umbrella, she was safe.

"My name is Professor Friedrich Bhaer," he said and handed her the last page.

"I'm Jo March," she said, still trembling from almost being run over. "Do you live at Mrs. Kirke's, too?"

The professor nodded, opened the front door for her, and followed her inside. "When first I saw you, I thought, 'Ah, she is a writer,'" he said.

Jo blushed. "What made you think so?" She took off her cloak and sat in a chair in the dining room.

The professor took her hand and pointed to her ink-stained fingers. "I know many writers. In Heidelberg, I was a professor at the university. Here, I am only a man with an accent." He offered Jo a cup of coffee. "You, too, are far from home, Miss March. You miss your family?"

"Yes, very much," Jo admitted. "Where is your wife, Professor?"

"I have no wife," he said and sipped his coffee. "I am a teacher. I take pupils and help them with their studies. I would like some day to see your work, if you would allow it."

Jo smiled, pleased. During the weeks that followed, Jo wrote late at night when Minnie and Kitty had gone to sleep. Finally, one day she received a letter from *The Weekly Volcano*. In excitement, she ran to tell the professor the good news. "The newspaper has taken two stories, and they wish to see more!" she said breathlessly.

"Wonderful!" he said. "May I?" He took the stories she held in her hand and began to read. Slowly, his happy expression changed to one of disappointment. "'The Sinner's Corpse' by Joseph March. You use another name?"

Jo nodded.

"They pay well I suppose?"

Jo felt crushed and angry at the same time. Why didn't he like what she had written? "People's lives are dull. They want thrilling stories," she said, her voice quavering.

The professor frowned. "People want whiskey, but I think you and I do not care to sell it." He cleared his throat and tapped the page with his finger. "This is a waste of your mind. You write of lunatics and vampires!"

"It will buy firewood for Marmee and Father, and a new coat for Beth, and she'll be grateful to have it," Jo said angrily. Tears filled her eyes. She grabbed the story and turned away. The professor gently took her arm to keep her from leaving.

"Please," he said. "I do not wish to insult you. Understand me. I am saying, you must please yourself. You must write about what you know, about what is important to you. I can see you have talent."

"You can?"

"Yes, but you should be writing something from your life, from the depths of your soul. There is more in you than this," he said, pointing to the newspaper story, "if you have the courage to write it."

Jo wiped her eyes and tucked the story inside the folder. She felt more hopeful. But what could she write about?

"Do not seem discouraged by this professor's words," he said and smiled. "I make a humble gift. An experience. Do you like the opera?"

Jo had never gone to an opera in her life. "I don't have a fancy dress," she said. "I don't see how I can go."

The professor put her cloak around her shoulders. "You are perfect. Where we are sitting, we will not be so formal."

That evening, the professor and Jo were ushered through the back door of the theater by one of the professor's friends, the stage manager. He showed them to their seats high above the stage. They perched among the scenery ropes and lighting.

Jo thought the opera was wonderful and felt enchanted as the love story unfolded. She was so busy watching the performance, she did not notice how tenderly the professor looked at her.

"I've never seen the city at this hour," she told him as they hurried back to Mrs. Kirke's in the falling snow. "Doesn't the snow look like falling stars?" The professor nodded, speechless. They had had a lovely evening together.

The enchantment was broken, however, when Jo left the professor and returned to her room. There she discovered a telegram slipped under the door. She quickly tore it open and read:

"Dear Jo. Beth is dying. Come home at once."

Jo packed her belongings. Early the next morning, she rushed to catch the next train home. She was in such a hurry, she did not even have time to say good-bye to the professor.

CHAPTER THIRTEEN

Amy Grows Up

While Jo hurried home, far across the ocean Amy was still unaware how serious Beth's illness had become. Amy traveled with Aunt March and worked on her painting whenever Aunt March allowed it. However, her aunt's main goal on their trip was to find a rich husband for Amy.

One day while painting a canvas in a garden, Amy was surprised by a familiar face. "Hello!" said Laurie, laughing. "I've been here in Nice for the past week or two."

Amy noticed Laurie's fashionable, messy clothing and the way he winked at all the women who passed by. He did not seem at all like the sincere, pleasant fellow she remembered as a little girl. Perhaps the gossip she had heard about him was correct. "I find you changed," she said disapprovingly.

Laurie smiled as if he did not care. "In fact, I despise you. You laze about spending your family's money and courting women. You aren't serious about studying music."

Laurie scowled. "My compositions are like your paintings. Mediocre copies of another man's genius."

Amy, stinging from his words, replied, "Then why don't you go to your grandfather in London and make yourself useful?"

"I should," he said and smiled. "Why don't you reform me?"

"I've someone more practical in mind," Amy said and described her latest suitor, a well-mannered young man who earned forty thousand dollars a year. "I didn't come to Europe to marry a poor man. I expect a proposal any day."

Laurie looked disappointed. "You'll regret it," he said, then added quietly, "I'll regret it. I am reminded of a promise. Didn't I say I would kiss you before you die?"

Amy turned away. "Do you hear from Jo? She has befriended a German professor. She has written me many letters about him."

"No doubt," Laurie said and laughed bitterly. "I envy her happiness. I envy his happiness. I envy John Brooke for marrying Meg. Just as you have always known you would not marry a poor man, I have always known that I should be part of the March family."

Amy sighed and suddenly felt sorry for Laurie. "I do not wish to be loved for my family."

"Any more than your suitor wishes to be loved for his money?" Laurie replied.

Angrily, Amy stood up and left. Later that afternoon, a letter arrived at Aunt March's apartment addressed to her. The letter was from Laurie. It said:

"...It is you I want, and not your family. I have gone to London, to make myself worthy of you. Please do not do anything we shall regret."

Amy folded the letter slowly and wondered when she would see Laurie again.

CHAPTER FOURTEEN

Beth's Wish

When Jo arrived from New York at her family's home, she ran up the muddy path. She was greeted by Meg.

"Why didn't you tell me you were expecting a baby?" Jo said happily.

Meg looked embarrassed. "One hardly speaks of these things."

"It's wonderful!" Jo said. "How's Beth?"

Meg's expression saddened. "You will find her very changed."

Jo hurried to Beth's room. She stood in the doorway, speechless. Beth's face was pale and thin. Her hands looked bony, her wrists fragile. As she slept, her mouth moved and her forehead wrinkled as if she were in pain.

Marmee joined Jo in the doorway. She, too, looked much changed. Her face was creased with worry. "She would not let us send for you sooner," she whispered to Jo. "We have had Dr. Bangs in so many times. But it is beyond all of us, now. Dear Beth is worn out with it. I don't know why she holds on."

Jo, moved by her mother's grief, hugged her. "There, there," she said. But she could not help feeling guilty that she had left her family and gone to New York.

All afternoon Jo sat by Beth's bedside. When she finally woke up, she offered her a cup of warmed broth. "You're going to drink all of this," she said.

Beth took a sip. Not once did her eyes leave Jo's face. "I'm glad you're home. I feel stronger with you close by."

Jo glanced at the cat that prowled about the room. "Old Mrs. Pat-Paw and I are going to get you well yet."

"If God wants me with Him, there is none who will stop Him," Beth said quietly. "I don't mind. I was never like the rest of you. Making plans about the great things I'd do. I never saw myself as anything much. Not a great writer, like you."

Jo sighed and bit her lip. "I'm not a great writer."

"But you will be," Beth said and smiled. "Oh, Jo, I've missed you so. Why does everyone want to go away? I love being home. But I don't like being left behind. Now I'm the one going ahead."

"Now, Beth—"

"I'm not afraid," Beth interrupted and gently patted Jo's hand. "I can be brave like you. The only hard part now is leaving you all. I know that I shall be homesick for you, even in Heaven."

Jo blinked hard to keep her tears from falling. "I won't let you go," she said fiercely. Suddenly, the cat crouched, arched its back, and stared at the window. "What is it, Mrs. Pat-Paw?" Wind moaned and rattled the pane. Jo stood and opened the window. The cat leapt to the sill and disappeared into the night.

As Jo locked the window, she turned to Beth. Her sister looked as if she were sleeping. One hand lay tucked beneath her cheek. Jo crept nearby. Why didn't her sister's frail shoulders rise and fall as she breathed? Jo watched. She waited. When she knew for certain that her sister had at last peacefully passed away, she took her hand—now as light as a feather. Filled with sorrow, Jo sat on the edge of the bed and cried and cried.

Beth's absence could be felt everywhere in the house. On the day of her funeral, a telegram came from Switzerland. Marmee, dressed in black, read the news aloud to Jo, Father, and Meg in the parlor:

"Aunt March is bedridden. Sea voyage not possible. I must come home later. All my love, Amy."

Marmee folded the telegram and put it back in her pocket. "I know Laurie will go to console Amy if he can."

"Laurie is in Switzerland?" Jo asked, surprised.

"Amy has written that he's become very successful working for his grandfather in London. She says he's visited her several times," Marmee replied.

Jo had never considered her sister and Laurie might have fallen in love. Her own feelings for Laurie had not changed. Perhaps it was for the best that he could comfort Amy while she was so far away from home. Jo took a deep breath and looked at her grief-stricken parents. "Will we never be all together again?"

Neither her mother nor her father answered.

For many weeks, Jo's sadness seemed almost too much to bear. She missed Beth, the one person who always listened to her problems, her dreams. Jo tried running in the woods. She visited the hedge where the birdhouse post office once perched. She walked along the pond and in the garden—all the haunts that used to make her happy. But nothing made her happy now.

One evening, she took a candle and went up to the attic. After so many months of neglect, the floor was dusty, the walls covered with cobwebs. Jo discovered in one corner a trunk with the word "Beth" printed in her sister's handwriting. She lifted the lid.

Inside, she found Beth's precious toys, her dolls, and a copy of the Pickwick Society newspaper. Jo was so moved, she began to cry. She wiped her eyes with her sleeve and looked about the cluttered attic. It seemed almost as if she could see and hear her sisters again as they performed their plays and created their games and adventures of long, long ago.

Jo found the paper, ink, and pen she had always kept in the attic. She lit a candle and sat at the table. Slowly she placed her velveteen writing cap on her head. She dipped her pen in the ink. And how the stories unfolded! Jo wrote on and on about happy times and sad times. As she wrote, it seemed to her as if at last she was able to bring them all together again. There they were—Meg, Jo, Beth, and Amy.

For the next several days, Jo wrote furiously, barely stopping to eat or sleep. When she was finished, she bound the pages together and wrapped them in brown paper. For once she had written about the people she knew best. She had written something from her life, from the depths of her soul.

Carefully, she printed in large letters on the front of the package:

Professor Bhaer
11 Waverly Place
New York City, New York

CHAPTER FIFTEEN

Autumn 1868
New Beginnings

Days turned to weeks, weeks to months. Jo did not return to New York City. Instead, she remained at home to help her sister with her twin babies, who were born that summer. She felt happy to be needed and appreciated by her family. But sometimes it seemed to her as if she were trapped in a cage. She felt restless and lonely. It did not seem fair that Amy and Meg should have all that they wished for while she had nothing.

One afternoon in late autumn, Jo kneaded bread dough in the kitchen. She looked out the window and watched the line filled with dozens of diapers dancing in the breeze. With her foot she rocked a cradle. Her sister bent over the sink to give the other baby a bath.

Meg noticed Jo's sad expression and tried to cheer her up. "What of your friend, the German in New York? I fancied, well, that you discussed more than books and opera with him." She chuckled when she saw the startled look on Jo's face.

"We were more than friends," Jo said and began to knead the dough faster. "I never said a proper good-bye to him. I'm a failure at romance I fear."

"John and I do not always agree. But then we mend it."

Jo shook her head as if her sister did not understand. "I sent him something—a book I wrote. And he did not respond."

"But if he did respond, and you could mend your misunderstanding, would you?"

Jo paused for a moment, deep in thought. "Sometimes," she said slowly, "I wish I had someone to love as you love John."

Suddenly, the front gate bell jingled. Jo wiped her floury hands on her apron and hurried to answer it. "Whoever could that be?" she muttered.

When she opened the hallway door, she was shocked to discover Laurie. He grinned bashfully beneath a proper grown-up mustache. "This is magic!" Jo said and gave him a friendly hug.

"You are absolutely covered with flour!" he exclaimed, laughing. "I have something for you."

"Should I call the others? The rest of the family's here in the kitchen, the garden—"

"Not yet," Laurie interrupted. "May I present my wife?" He opened the door wider and gently pulled into view—

Amy.

She grinned shyly at Jo. Would she be welcome?

Jo, speechless, looked at Amy as if she had seen a ghost. Was her sister actually standing there before her? "Amy!" Jo said joyfully. She threw her arms around her and kissed her.

"You must tell me the truth as my sister, which is a relation stronger than marriage," Amy said quietly, staring intently into Jo's eyes. "Do you mind at all that Laurie and I are married?"

"I am surprised," Jo admitted and then took both of their hands. She looked happily at Laurie. "At last we're all family, as we should have been. Tell me that you and Amy will always live close by. I could not bear losing another sister."

CHAPTER SIXTEEN

A Surprise in the Rain

That winter, Aunt March died. Jo was astonished when her aunt gave her Plumfield Estate in her will. She had not expected such generosity. One afternoon, Jo, her sisters, and Marmee wandered about the abandoned house. The furniture was covered with sheets. The place smelled dusty, closed-up.

Marmee, holding Aunt March's poodle in one arm, drew back the shutters. The enormous dining room flooded with sunlight. "One would require quite an income just to heat this place. What could Aunt March have been thinking?"

Jo ran her finger along the rows and rows of leather-bound books lining the shelves in the next room. "Most likely she felt sorry for me. A homeless spinster. Poor Aunt! Living here all those years, alone in this useless place."

Marmee opened the drapes in the library and gazed about the room. "People with money never seem to know what to do with it. Wouldn't this make a wonderful school?"

Jo turned thoughtfully. "A school?"

"What a great undertaking that would be," Marmee said.

Jo sighed. "Too great for one person."

Finally, spring arrived. Late one rainy afternoon, Jo burst through the kitchen door of her family's house. Her coat and hat were soaked. She laughed as Aunt March's poodle skittered and barked its greeting. As she bent over to yank off her muddy boots, she noticed something on the table. A parcel.

When she looked more closely she saw something strange. In her own handwriting on the damp brown parcel were written the words:

Friedrich Bhaer
11 Waverly Place
New York City, New York

Eagerly she tore open the paper. Inside, she discovered pages from a new book. On the first page, in bold print it said, "A novel by Josephine March. James T. Fields, Publishers, New York."

Jo howled with delight. She raced into the dining room. "Hannah!" she shouted, "someone is publishing my book."

"Heaven take us!" Hannah replied and gave Jo a great hug.

"There's no letter. How did it arrive?" Jo asked. She showed her the brown parcel.

"Foreign gentleman brought it. Strange kind of name. Can't think of it. Fox or Bear or such."

"Was it Bhaer?"

Hannah shrugged. "Seemed refined for a delivery person. He said he had a train to catch."

Jo gazed desperately around the kitchen, searching for some other clue, some other sign that the professor had actually been there. Behind the door she noticed a familiar object. The professor's big battered black umbrella!

She grabbed the umbrella and bolted out the door.

"Where are you going?" Hannah called.

"The train station!" Jo shouted. She rushed down the lane. What if she was too late? She ran faster. At each corner, she peered in all directions. No one. Where had he gone?

She hurried on, only a block from the train station. There, in the distance, she caught sight of a tall shape—the professor carrying his carpetbag. "Friedrich!" Jo shouted, waving to him with the umbrella. Her face shone with happiness. "Thank you for my book." She hugged him.

He returned her embrace. "Reading it was like opening a window and looking into your heart."

Embarrassed, Jo looked away for a moment. "When I didn't hear from you, I thought you hated it."

"No, no. It's just that I've been away lecturing in many places. After you left New York, I made myself very busy. But when I came back and found your wonderful manuscript, I had to show it to Fields, the publisher. I could not keep such a book to myself."

"I can't thank you enough." She handed him the umbrella.

The professor opened it over them. "I did nothing. James Fields took it out of my hands and wouldn't give it back. I thought, 'Such news I should tell her myself.' It was a silly impulse."

Jo took his arm. "Not silly at all. It's so good to see you. Come and meet my family. I've told my sisters so much about you."

The professor shook his head. "Please apologize to them, but I have only a short time between trains. I am going out West."

"West?" Jo said, stunned.

"The schools are young there. They don't mind a different way of teaching. And I fear there is nothing to keep me here." He took her hand formally. "So we will say good-bye?"

Jo gulped. She felt as if the wind had been knocked out of her. "It—it was kind of you to bring me news of my book."

The professor nodded and began to walk away. Then he stopped. "It was selfish. I thought, perhaps she will say, 'Friedrich, don't go so far away.' Though I know that you could never need me as I have needed you."

Jo ran to him. "That isn't true!" she exclaimed. "Friedrich, I've never wanted to be with anyone as I want to be with you. Please don't go so far away."

The professor put down his carpetbag, his face suddenly filled with hope.

"Say you'll stay here," Jo continued, "and let us make a wonderful life together."

"I will, of course, I will. But I have nothing to give you. My hands are empty."

Jo put her hands tenderly in his. "Not empty now." Under the battered umbrella, they kissed. The professor picked up his carpetbag and together they walked through the mud and rain to her family's house. Outside the doorway, he shook the umbrella and closed it gently. The umbrella flapped, sounding like the wings of a landing bird. "Welcome home," Jo said and led the professor inside.